Laffite the Pirate

BY
ARIANE DEWEY

A MULBERRY PAPERBACK BOOK, NEW YORK

FOR THE SUZETTES

Library of Congress Cataloging-in-Publication Data
Dewey, Ariane.
Laffite, the pirate / by Ariane Dewey.
p.   cm.
Summary: Presents sheer myths and some stories
based in fact about the controversial pirate
who aided the United States in the War of 1812,
but returned to his life of piracy thereafter.
ISBN 0-688-04578-2
1. Laffite, Jean—Juvenile fiction. 2. Children's
stories, American.[1. Laffite, Jean—Fiction.
2. Pirates—Fiction.]   I. Title.
[PZ7.D5228Laf 1993]   [E]—dc20
92-43787   CIP AC

CONTENTS

1. RASCALS AND TROUBLEMAKERS

Jean Laffite was the captain of the *Ninette*.
Rascals and troublemakers were his crew.
Their first victim was a merchant ship,
the *Bristol Mary*.

It was big and the *Ninette* was tiny,
but that didn't stop Laffite.
He fired a warning shot
across its bow.

"We're being attacked by a bathtub,"
sneered the British crew, and fired.
But not one of the *Bristol Mary*'s six
cannons could hit the target.

"There's something strange here,"
  said the British captain,
  and away they sailed.
  Laffite chased after them
  and came alongside.
  He and his pirates leaped aboard,
  slashing their cutlasses and
  firing their pistols.
  The British were so surprised
  they surrendered.

"Laffite thanks you for your ship!"
said her proud new captain.

It wasn't long before they sighted the *Pagoda*.
Laffite pretended the *Bristol Mary* was an
English pilot ship.
He offered to guide the *Pagoda* into port.
The *Pagoda* accepted.
Laffite signaled he was bringing them
a navigator.

Instead, he and his men jumped aboard.
They aimed pistols and daggers at the
Pagoda's unarmed crew.
"Surrender!" ordered Laffite.
They did.

Laffite sold the *Bristol Mary*, the *Pagoda*,
and all their cargo.
And he bought *La Confiance*, a sleek sloop.
He armed her with twenty-six cannons.
Two hundred cutthroats were his crew.

"Now I will capture whomever I please
for mine will be the fastest ship
on the seas," he swore.
Then he sailed out to find the *Queen*,
the largest merchant ship afloat.
One day, there she was with her forty
guns and four hundred men.
Laffite opened fire.

"What impudence!"
said the *Queen*'s
captain.
And he let go
a broadside.
It missed.

Laffite maneuvered alongside the *Queen*.
His men tossed iron balls filled with
gunpowder up onto the *Queen*'s deck.

"They're throwing stones at us,"
the *Queen*'s crew said, laughing.

But the iron balls exploded. Men were thrown
overboard and Laffite captured the *Queen*.
He took his loot and sailed for New Orleans.

2. THE TERROR OF THE GULF

There is a maze of bayous and swamps
between New Orleans and the Gulf of Mexico
called Barataria.
It was a hideout for smugglers.
People called them the Baratarians,
and Jean Laffite became their leader.

"I don't take orders from anyone,"
a vicious pirate bragged.

"Too bad," said Laffite, and he
shot him dead. "I'm boss here!"
No one argued.

The captured cargoes were unloaded
at a hidden harbor.
Laffite held auctions to sell
whatever the ships brought.
Merchants and planters came from all
over Louisiana to look for bargains.
Prices were low because there were
no import taxes to pay.

The next day a new proclamation appeared.

I, Boss of
BARATARIA
offer a
REWARD
of
$5000
to anyone who delivers
Governor William Claiborne
to me
Jean Laffite

The Governor at once sent troops
to Barataria.
"Destroy that pirate's nest and seize
those thieving scoundrels!" he ordered.

But instead of fighting,
Laffite invited the soldiers to dinner.

Afterward he loaded them with treasure
and sent them back to the governor
with his compliments.
"New Orleans is such a dull place,"
Laffite grumbled.
And he sailed off to Galveston.

3. THE TIDAL WAVE

In 1818 a hurricane roared out of the Gulf.
It uprooted trees and blew away houses.
Laffite ordered his ships out to sea
to weather the storm.

Galveston Island was covered with water.
"You can flood the land,
    but you can't hurt me,"
Laffite shouted into the wind.
Just then a tidal wave picked up his ship
and hurled it toward the rocky shore.

Laffite hoisted his sails and rode
the crest of the wave.
It carried the ship straight over the
island and halfway across Texas.
The men cheered.
"What a ride!" Laffite shouted.

31

4. BURIED TREASURE

Laffite captured so much treasure
he didn't know what to do with it.
He stuffed coins into cannons,
sealed the barrels,
and dumped them overboard.

He sank gold
in the swamps
of Barataria.
He hid handfuls
of jewels
in Galveston.

He buried trunks of treasure all along
the coasts of Louisiana and Texas.
Then he vanished.
People have been searching for his
booty ever since.
Nothing has been found.

Rumor had it that Laffite had buried
a trunk full of gold in a salt grass
meadow near the Lavaca River. It was said
a brass rod marked the spot.
One day a boy was herding sheep.
It was hot and he felt sleepy.

He was looking around for something
to tie his horse to, when he
stubbed his toe.
There was a brass rod sticking out
of the ground. He looped the reins
around it and took a nap.

When he awoke, he pulled up the strange stake and took it along to show his father. When his father saw the rod, he jumped up and down crying, "We're rich, rich, rich! This is Laffite's marker for sure!"

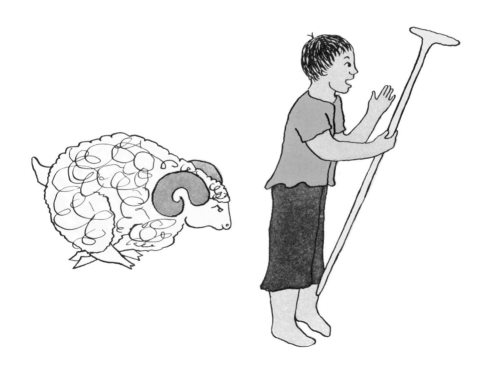

But the boy couldn't remember just
where he'd found it.
For weeks they poked and prodded
and dug over every foot of that meadow
and never turned up a thing.

5. GHOSTS

Some say Laffite's treasure is haunted.
Once a man heard of a place where
it might be buried.
He thought it best to dig at night.
It was just past midnight.
He dug down about six feet.

Suddenly he heard a crowing and
squawking.
Up came a rooster in a puff of smoke
and was gone.

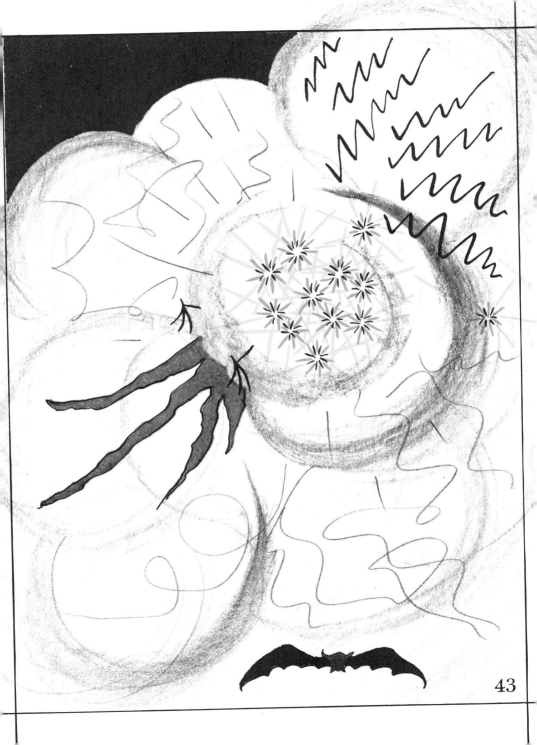

43

Next came a screeching, ghostly cat.
She too disappeared.

Then a horse came trotting right
out of the ground.
He was breathing smoke, and fire
came out of his eyes and ears.
The man ran for his life.

The treasure stayed where it was,
and is there still for anyone to find—
that is, anyone who's not afraid of ghosts.